AF594428

BLUE Banner BIOGRAPHIES

DONOVAN MITCHELL

John Bankston

PUBLISHERS

2001 SW 31st Avenue
Hallandale, FL 33009

www.mitchelllane.com

First Edition, 2020.
Author: John Bankston
Designer: Ed Morgan
Editor: Lisa Petrillo

Series: Blue Banner Biographies
Title: Donovan Mitchell / by John Bankston

Hallandale, FL : Mitchell Lane Publishers, [2020]

Library bound ISBN: 9781883845995
eBook ISBN: 9781584150428

PHOTO CREDITS: Design Elements, freepik.com, Getty Images, p. 15 Fletcher6 CC-BY-SA-3.0

Contents

CHAPTER **ONE**

Waiting

ALL DONOVAN MITCHELL could do was watch. He was 16 years old. It was the July before his junior year in high school.

Every summer, sneaker companies sponsor games where high school basketball players show off their skills to top college coaches. It's a huge opportunity to be chosen for athletic glory. Hundreds of talented high school players dream of playing in college. Few make it. Unfortunately, Donovan was on the sidelines.

In March, he'd become injured playing baseball at Canterbury School in New Milford, Connecticut. "I ran into my catcher trying to catch a pop fly," Donovan told a reporter with the *Deseret News*. "We ran into each other when I was playing shortstop and he actually ended up breaking his jaw and I broke my wrist."

The injury ended his season. It wouldn't end his dreams. When he traveled with his team to the tournaments, "I was in a cast." he told a reporter from *The New York Post*. "I had to sit and watch my team play, and sometimes they would lose." Growing up, he'd loved baseball. In high school, he realized he loved basketball more. The injury helped him make a decision. "That was the last straw," he told *The Post*. He stopped playing baseball.

In high school, Donovan Mitchell focused on basketball.

Not being able to compete in the sneaker tournaments meant most college coaches had not seen him play and didn't know who he was. The top high school players are ranked. Donovan wasn't even on the list of top players. He wanted to change that.

He decided to leave home and move to New Hampshire for his final two years of high school, to attend a school famous for its star athletes. "When he arrived here, he didn't have a number next to his name or a national ranking," Jason Smith, the school's coach told a reporter for *The New York Times* in 2017. "He was hungry."

Waiting

Most people wouldn't want to leave friends and family behind to chase a dream. His father, who had played basketball while he was in high school, wasn't surprised. "When he spends time in the gym and puts his mind to what he wants accomplished, he gets it done," Donovan Mitchell Sr. told *The Post* in June 2017. Both Donovans may have had playing basketball in common. But Donovan Jr. grew up with a baseball-loving dad who had once chased his own major league dreams.

A player's wingspan is the length between the fingertips of each outstretched arm. Mitchell has a 6'10" wingspan.

CHAPTER **TWO**

A Different Path

PLAYING PROFESSIONAL SPORTS is hard. Most people play sports for fun. Being a professional is different. It's more competitive. The stakes are higher. And it's not easy making a living.

Top players earn millions of dollars. Yet most professional athletes make less than they would at a regular job. They do it because they love the game.

Major League Baseball has a farm league. Just like farms grow crops, farm leagues grow players. These minor league teams are where professional baseball players start their careers. Most end them there as well. They play for teams like the South Carolina RiverDogs. The most talented go on to play for Major League teams like the Boston Red Sox. Donovan Mitchell Sr. was one of the many who never did.

Donovan's father was drafted by the Houston Astros in 1992. For the next seven seasons, he played with the team's minor league clubs. He reached Class AAA in 1998. It was the highest level in the minors. Many players go from triple-A to the Major Leagues. Instead, the next year he retired.

CHAPTER **TWO**

His son carried both his name and his pro ball dreams. Donovan Corey Mitchell Jr. was born on September 7, 1996, in Elmsford, New York. Although he never saw his father play, he was able to see plenty of pro baseball because of his father's job. Donovan Sr. was a coach for the New York Mets' minor league clubs. Today he is the Mets Director of Player Relations.

"He'd go to all the Mets games, come down and spend time with me during spring training and when I was managing, he would get on the bus with me and ride to different games," Donovan Sr. told a reporter for the *Deseret News* in May 2018. Growing up, Donovan Jr. visited the Columbia, South Carolina, clubhouse where his father was coaching, and took batting practice in Norfolk, Virginia.

Being able to see top players helped him realize how hard they worked. It was a lesson his father believed he learned well. He told a reporter for the *New York Post* that his son had dreamed of being a pro athlete as "a little kid. [Donovan] works hard. Sacrificed a lot. I like best how humble he is and he puts his team and teammates first." Despite Donovan Sr.'s background, "He fell in love with basketball like I fell in love with baseball." In the beginning, Donovan played both.

A Different Path

Elmsford is in Westchester County. It's a place known for quiet streets and tree-shaded homes. Every day, people like his dad took trains to work in nearby New York City. The family soon moved to Greenwich, Connecticut. It was a lot like Westchester, filled with people who traveled to New York City for their jobs but preferred a quieter place for home. Donovan and his sister Jordan attended a private school named Greenwich Country Day School. His mother, Nicole, taught preschool. Although he played baseball and basketball, he explained on the school's website that he learned more than athletic skills. "It's not all about winning. It's about caring for your teammates and helping everybody get better."

CHAPTER TWO

A Different Path

At Greenwich, he became a star pitcher. Teammate Parker Holbrook told a reporter for the *Deseret News* that Donovan "threw two or three no hitters" when he was in eighth grade. By the time he was in high school playing for Canterbury School, his fastball approached 90 mph.

Playing two sports was ideal. Baseball kept him busy in the spring. Basketball became his focus in the winter. After his injury on the center field in tenth grade, that life he loved changed.

His parents agreed with his choice to move to New Hampshire and attend a boarding school famous for its sports. He knew the top colleges barely knew who he was. He also knew he didn't have much time to change that.

CHAPTER **THREE**

Leaving Home

NEW HAMPSHIRE is one of the smallest states in the country. Twice as many people live in Brooklyn, New York. Yet it is home to some of the best-known schools in the world.

Boarding schools are a lot like college. They are private schools whose students live and study away from home. Fourteen of the state's top boarding schools educate more than 4,000 students. Former Secretary of State John Kerry attended St. Paul's School in Concord while Phillips Exeter Academy in Exeter counts Facebook founder Mark Zuckerberg amongst its graduates.

Brewster Academy in Wolfeboro began as the town's only high school in 1820. Today it offers a tech-savvy education, providing laptops to arriving freshmen. They not only use them to communicate but for posting online portfolios throughout their high school career. Brewster is also known as a basketball powerhouse. So impressive are the results of its program that in the past ten years, ten of its students have gone on to play in the National Basketball Association.

Brewster Academy in Wolfeboro, New Hampshire

CHAPTER **THREE**

After Donovan Mitchell arrived, he didn't waste time. He spent hours practicing dunks. He would bounce the ball off the backboard or the wall of the gym. He would shoot it through his legs at the foul line. As a guard, he gave himself a goal to keep the highest-scoring player on the other team from scoring no more than ten points. He usually met his goal.

He helped Brewster Academy to achieve a winning record. The first season his team didn't lose a single game. The second, they only lost one.

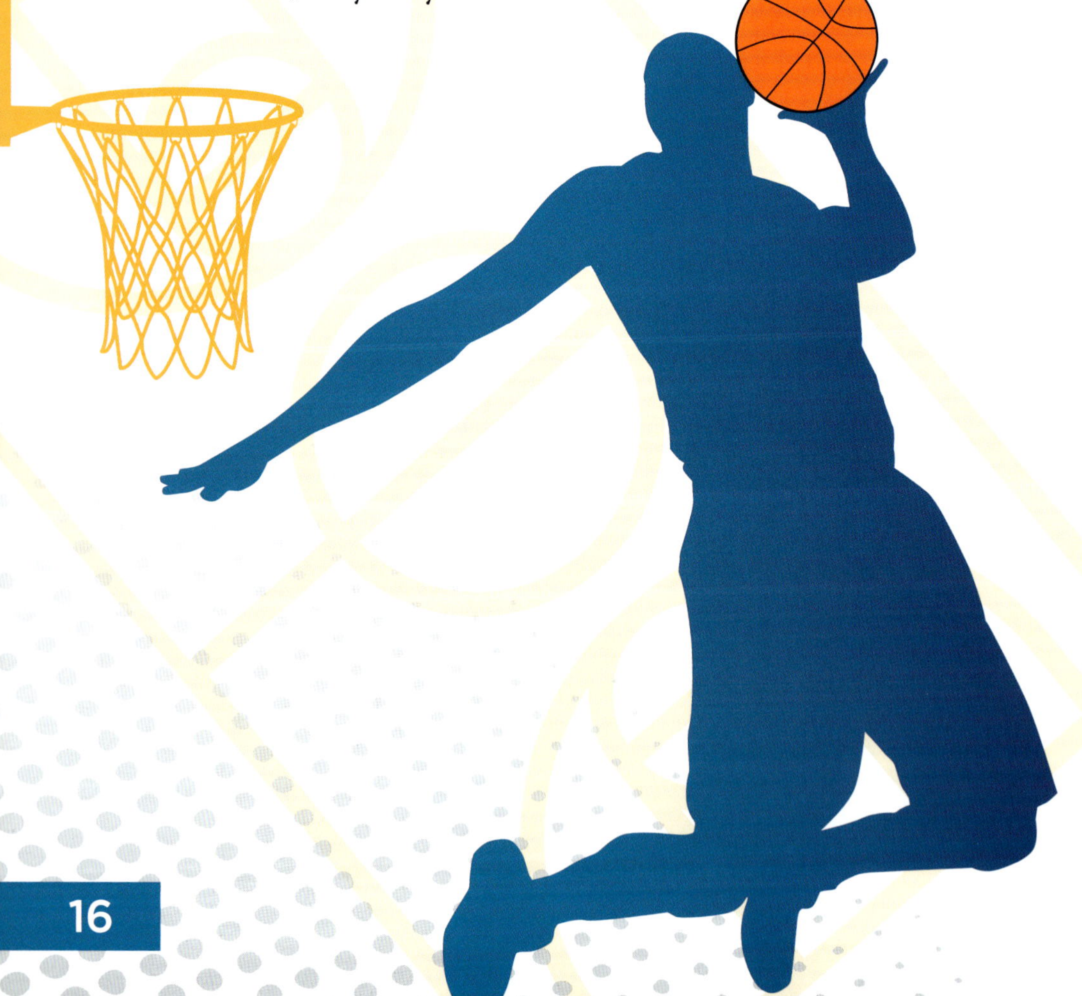

Leaving Home

During the summers, he returned to play games in New York City. The first time he dunked it was on a slanted court in New York's Harlem. The slant helped him reach the rim.

The Amateur Athletic Union (AAU) began in 1888 and today has more 700,000 students playing basketball, volleyball, and many other sports. Even as Donovan went to other schools, he continued playing guard for both The City and the Riverside Hawks AAU teams. It's where he earned his nickname, "Spida D" for the way he guarded the net, with seemingly as many arms as a spider.

At first, he didn't stand out. He was shorter than many players. In their early teens, top basketball players are often well over six feet tall. Even as an adult, Donovan would only be 6'1 in his socks (6'3 in shoes). Until his junior year, he was skinny. And as he told a reporter for the *Daily News*, "I couldn't shoot, I couldn't dribble—I was just a dunker. I played defense and dunked. That's it."

Mitchell stands 6'3" with shoes on.

CHAPTER **THREE**

To The City's coach, it wasn't a player's talent or size that mattered. "He has a ton of character," Arjay Perovic explained to *The New York Post*. "He wants to do what's right. Donovan was the heart of our program. Not only is Donovan a great basketball player, but he's a better kid. He's a leader."

He led The City to an AAU National Championship in 2012. At Brewster Academy, he helped his team win two national championships. His senior year, he was elected class president.

After just one year at Brewster, everything had changed. His wrist was healed. His skills were sharpened. And top college recruiters were paying attention.

During a little over one week in July he traveled to Philadelphia, Pennsylvania, for the Reebok Breakout Classic camp, and competed with The City in Springfield, Massachusetts, for the BasketBull Summer Championships and the UAA Finals in Atlanta, Georgia. That month he told a reporter for the *New York Post*, "I just want to be able to showcase my game. Coming into this month I'm an unknown."

He wasn't unknown for long. Soon after the games he had scholarship offers from the Georgetown University, in Washington, D.C., University of Florida, and Xavier University in Ohio. Other top colleges like St. John's University in the New York City borough of Queens, and Florida State University were also interested.

Leaving Home

His mother, Nicole Mitchell, was less interested in the sport than the opportunity. "I thought, 'Jackpot, we've got a good education ahead of us,'" she told *Slam* online basketball magazine.

In August 2014, Donovan announced he would enroll at the University of Louisville. The Kentucky school's head coach, Rick Pitino, admitted that it was his son who first told him about the skills of the guard from Greenwich. "I said, 'Ryan, there are just children of [bankers] in Greenwich. There are no basketball players in Greenwich," he told a reporter for the *Courier-Journal* that November. Donovan Mitchell soon proved him wrong.

Although many college teams recruited Donovan Mitchell, he chose to play for the top-ranked University of Louisville Cardinals.

CHAPTER FOUR

Choices

COLLEGE BASKETBALL PLAYERS dream about a March Madness victory. Every spring, the nation's top teams enter the National Collegiate Athletic Association (NCAA) tournament. The 68 teams are culled to the "Sweet Sixteen," the "Elite Eight," and then the "Final Four." Usually the tournament's winner is a top-ranked team like University of California-Los Angeles or Duke University. Sometimes lesser-known programs win. This adds to the excitement.

During his freshman year, the closest Donovan Mitchell got to March Madness was playing the Tournament's video game. The Louisville Cardinals played in the NCAA Tournament nine years in a row. The Cardinals enjoyed four straight Sweet 16s and two Final Fours. In 2013, they won the championship. During the 2015 season they were ranked 16 with a 23-8 record. It didn't matter.

After admitting to breaking an NCAA rule, the Kentucky school decided not to enter the 2016 tournament. The team's 2013 win was erased as well. During the March 2017 tournament, Donovan told a reporter for the *New York Post*, "We didn't want to believe it. It was such a big shock." Worse, he learned about the decision after the Cardinals had beaten North Carolina, the number two team in the country. "A lot of us, we didn't know how to handle it. It hurt a lot. All we talked about was, 'Man, we should be there. That should be us.'"

Basketball's top freshmen get a lot of playing time. That's because, unlike other sports, the players often don't stay long. In 2005, the NBA began requiring players to be at least 19 before they could be drafted into professional leagues. Because players could no longer turn pro right after high school, they stayed in college for just one year. But after his freshman season, Mitchell realized he wasn't ready. He asked Coach Rick Pitino what he needed to do to turn pro.

"I said, 'Look, Donovan, you're a freak athlete, but if you're serious about this game, you have to get a jump shot with arc and really develop it,'" Pitino told a reporter for the *New York Post* in May 2017. And Mitchell listened. "I haven't seen a guy improve his jump shot more than him in my 40 years of coaching."

The next season, Mitchell excelled. So did his team. The Cardinals finished the year ranked eight with a 24-7 record. They did it despite losing the team's top three scorers. Focusing on defense, the team transformed. So did Mitchell. He went from being the team's fifth highest scorer to the top one.

As the team prepared for March Madness, he told a reporter for the *New York Post* in March 2017, "This team can accomplish anything because of their attitude."

Sports writers weren't the only people watching Donovan Mitchell. Pro teams were following him as well. The son of the Utah Jazz's General Manager Dennis Lindsey played for Baylor University. He noticed when Louisville took on the team during the 2016 championship game of the Battle 4 Atlantis in the Bahamas. Although Baylor came from 20 points down to win the game, Mitchell scored 17 points, eight rebounds and four assists.

After his second season with Louisville, he announced he would enter the draft. The next step was the workout.

College players who hope to turn pro travel to various teams. On May 27, 2017, he worked out with the Utah Jazz. He played against top college players like Kansas's Frank Mason and Amile Jefferson from Duke University. The Jazz's coaches didn't think he would play for the team. Utah had the 24th pick in the first round of the draft. Mitchell would probably be long gone by then.

Mitchell didn't care. "My biggest thing was I wanted to work out for every team in the first round," he told a reporter for *The Washington Post* in 2018. "That was my goal, just because I'm not one of those guys who looks for a promise, or a guarantee, you know?"

Working out for the Utah Jazz changed his future. "I'm not even sure the kid knew that he was performing to the degree that he was performing," Jazz General Manager Dennis Lindsey told *The Washington Post*.

Utah started trading. The Nuggets had the 13th pick. They traded Jazz player Trey Lyles for the slot. Although both the Charlotte Hornets and Detroit Pistons had been interested in Mitchell, they chose other players. The Jazz got Donovan Mitchell as the 13th pick. The 12 teams that passed him over would soon regret it.

Mitchell wears the number 45, honoring basketball great Michael Jordan.

CHAPTER FIVE

Top Rookie

TURNING PRO usually means spending a lot of time warming the bench. Donovan Mitchell might have wished he spent less time on the court. "We've put a lot on him, and he's capable of handling it. But I don't think he came into the year thinking he'd be playing as many minutes at the point as he's playing," admitted Jazz coach Quin Snyder to a reporter for the *New York Post* in November 2017.

By then, Mitchell had scored 26 points in a game against the New York Nets. Before the season ended, he would score over 40 points in a pair of games. After Orlando Magic forward Aaron Gordon was injured, Mitchell took his place in the 2018 NBA Slam Dunk Contest. He won—scoring a 48 and 50 in the first round and a 50 and 48 in the final round.

In April, he led his team to the playoffs against the Oklahoma City Thunder on April 15th. In his first game he scored 27 points. In his second, 28. He went on to set a record for points by a shooting guard in the post season. Although the Jazz defeated the Thunder four games to two, the team's post-season play ended when the Houston Rockets beat them four games to one. Still, it was an incredible accomplishment for Mitchell's first season. Although he lost Rookie of the Year to 76ers rookie point guard Ben Simmons, he was named to the NBA All-Rookie First Team.

Mitchell shows off his skills on Team USA during the NBA All-Star Rising Stars Challenge Game.

CHAPTER **FIVE**

Jazz fans were impressed by Donovan Mitchell's talent on the court. But everyone seemed to be impressed with what he did off of it.

At local Kearns High in Salt Lake City, he was the surprise guest. Some 300 students with the highest grades gathered for the start of the year assembly. Student Mauricio Izarraraz was stunned. "My brother's going to be so jealous," he told a reporter from *Deseret News* in August 2018. Still Izarraraz had to explain who Mitchell was to some classmates. "I didn't really know who he was until (Izarraraz) told me, but I think it's really cool," student Alondra Delgadillo told the news reporter. She even loaned the basketball player a marker so he could autograph T-shirts and nabbed a prize souvenir for herself.

In addition to visits around Salt Lake, Donovan also returned home. That June he ran a basketball camp for boys and girls in Greenwich. He even refereed 5-on-5 games, assisted by fellow basketball star Frank Ntilikina, who was drafted by the New York Knicks five spots ahead of Donovan.

"My biggest thing was, after the end of the season, was to have a camp, back here at GCS (Greenwich Country Day School), they did so much for me as a child," Mitchell told a reporter for the *Daily News*. "They helped my mom out, they helped my sister (Jordan) when she went here. I just wanted to give back. That's all I love doing is giving back to kids.

Right now it's just here, things will hopefully change throughout my years in the NBA, God willing, just finding a way to continue to give back to the community, to give my advice to kids about my story, because my story is unique." It's a story basketball fans hope to see played out for years to come.

Donovan Mitchell is known as a player who always has time for his fans—often signing autographs for everyone who asks.

Timeline

1996 Born September 7 in Elmsford, New York to Nicole and Donovan Mitchell Sr.

2012 Attends Greenwich Country Day School in Greenwich, Connecticut

2013 Attends Canterbury School in New Milford, Connecticut

2013 Transfers to Brewster Academy boarding school in Wolfeboro, N.H.

2014 Announces he will attend University of Louisville, Kentucky, and play basketball for its championship team, the Cardinals

2015 Graduates from Brewster Academy. Begins playing for the Cardinals, wearing Michael Jordan's number, 45

2017 Enters the NBA draft. Picked in the 13th round by the Utah Jazz

2018 Wins Slam Dunk Contest and almost wins Rookie of the Year

Selected Stats

High School

2012 AAU National Championship (The City)

2013-14 Brewster Academy, 33-0

2014-15 Brewster Academy, 34-1

2014, 2015 National Prep champions (Brewster Academy)

University of Louisville Kentucky

2015 Averaged 7.4 points per game
1.7 assists

2016 Averaged 15.6 points per game
2.7 assists per game

Utah Jazz

2017 Games Played: 79
Games started: 71
Points Per Game: 20.9
Free Throw Percentage: .805
Three-point percentage: 340

Selected Awards

2017 First-team All-ACC (All-Atlantic Coast)

2018 NBA All-Rookie First Team

2018 NBA Slam Dunk Contest champion

Find Out More

Books

Clausen-Grace, Nick. *Basketball superstars*. Chicago, IL: World Book, Inc., 2018.

Nagelhout, Ryan. *Basketball: Who Does What?* New York, NY : Gareth Stevens Publishing, 2018.

Omoth, Tyler. *Who's Who of Pro Basketball: a Guide to the Game's Greatest Players.* North Mankato, Minnesota: Capstone Press: 2016.

On the Internet

Learn about Donovan Mitchell's basketball camp
www.myway45.com

Learn more about sports programs at the AAU
http://aausports.org/About-AAU

Stats

http://www.nba.com/players/donovan/mitchell/1628378
https://www.basketball-reference.com/players/m/mitchdo01.html

Utah Jazz

https://www.nba.com/jazz/

Works Consulted

Periodicals

Barrow, Eric & Bondy, Stefan. "Frank helps at Mitchell's youth camp, *New York Daily News*. June 4, 2018.

Berman, Marc. "Point of Sale: Pitino: Cards' Mitchell can help Knicks at PG." *The New York Post*. May 26, 2017.

Bondy, Stefan. "Donovan Mitchell, who Knicks could've drafted, has changed game since AAU days in NYC," *The Daily News*. February 17, 2018. http://www.nydailynews.com/sports/basketball/knicks/donovan-mitchel-changed-game-aau-days-nyc-article-1.3825988.

Bontemps, Tim. "Jazz's Donovan Mitchell Exceeds Expectations," *The Washington Post*. May 7, 2018.

"Christmas in July: Mitchell Thrilled for Second Chance after Injury," *The New York Post*. July 19, 2014.

"Don's New Day!" *The New York Post*. June 7, 2017.

Genessy, Jody. *Deseret News*. [Salt Lake City, Utah] August 21, 2018.

Jones, Steve. "Pitino says he's satisfied with Cards' signing day," *Courier - Journal* [Louisville, Ky] November 18, 2014.

Landrigan, Kevin. "NH's Population Growth Leads the Northeast Region," *New Hampshire Union Leader*. September 5, 2018. http://www.unionleader.com/social-issues/nhs-population-growth-leads-the-northeast-region--20180905.

"Major deals," *Moose Jaw Times Herald* [Moose Jaw, Saskatchewan.] January 2000.

"Prohibited from Postseason Play a year ago, Cardinals ready to roll," *The New York Post*. March 7, 2017.

Vorkunov, Mike. "N.B.A. Prospect Knows What It's Like to Be a Pro (but in Baseball)," *New York Times*. June 23, 2017.

Woodyard, Eric. *Deseret News*. [Salt Lake City, Utah] May 8, 2018.

Web Sites

"Alumni: The City" https://thecitybball.org/new-page-1/

"Character," Greenwich Country Day School. https://www.gcds.net/about/headmasters-welcome/character

Figman, Adam. Jazz Rookie Donovan Mitchell is a Ready-Made Superstar, *Slam-online*. March 21, 2018. https://www.slamonline.com/nba/donovan-mitchell-slam-cover/

"Top New Hampshire Boarding Schools," https://www.boardingschoolreview.com/new-hampshire

Index

About the Author

Born in Boston, Massachusetts, John Bankston began writing professionally while still a teenager. Bankston is the author of more than 100 nonfiction books for children and young adults, including Mitchell Lane biographies of Abby Wambach, Kevin Durant and Selena Gomez. His favorite part of writing biographies like this one, is writing about the challenges the subjects faced and how they overcome them. Often the challenge—like Donovan Mitchell's broken wrist—changed the direction of their life.